W9-BGR-058

A B C
Toy Chest

by David Korr · Illustrated by Nancy W. Stevenson

Featuring Jim Henson's Sesame Street Muppets

A SESAME STREET/GOLDEN PRESS BOOK

Published by Western Publishing Company, Inc.
in conjunction with Children's Television Workshop.

©1981 Children's Television Workshop. Muppet characters © 1981 Muppets, Inc. All rights reserved. Printed in U.S.A. SESAME STREET®, the SESAME STREET SIGN, and SESAME STREET BOOK CLUB are trademarks and service marks of Children's Television Workshop. GOLDEN® and GOLDEN PRESS® are trademarks of Western Publishing Company, Inc. No part of this book may be reproduced or copied in any form without written permission from the publisher. Library of Congress Catalog Card Number: 80-84192 ISBN 0-307-23129-1

Herry is looking for something
in his toy chest.
What do you suppose it is?

Well, it's not his accordion.

Accordion

Barbell

It's not his barbell.

It's not his camera...

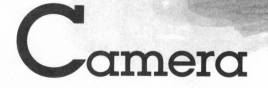

Camera

...or his dandy dancing doll.

Doll

It's not his toy elephant, either.

Elephant

Is it his fire truck, or his galoshes?

Fire truck

Galoshes

Is it his hat?

Hat

Iron

Jacket

No, and it's not his iron or the jacket
he wears when he goes roller-skating.

Is Herry looking for his lamp,
or his mailbox with a nest inside?

Lamp

Mailbox

Nest

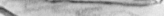

Or his old orange owl?

Owl

His paperbag puppet?

Puppet

What is he looking for?
It's clearly not his quilt.

Quilt

And it's not his radio.

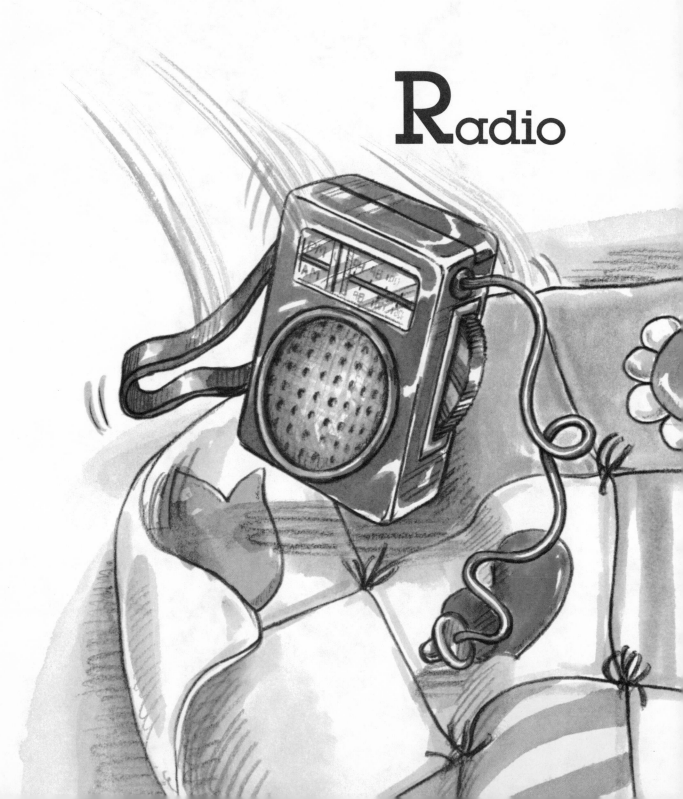

Radio

It's not his toy stove.

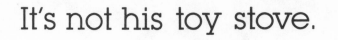

Stove

Or his tambourine. And there goes his
long underwear. It's not that, either.

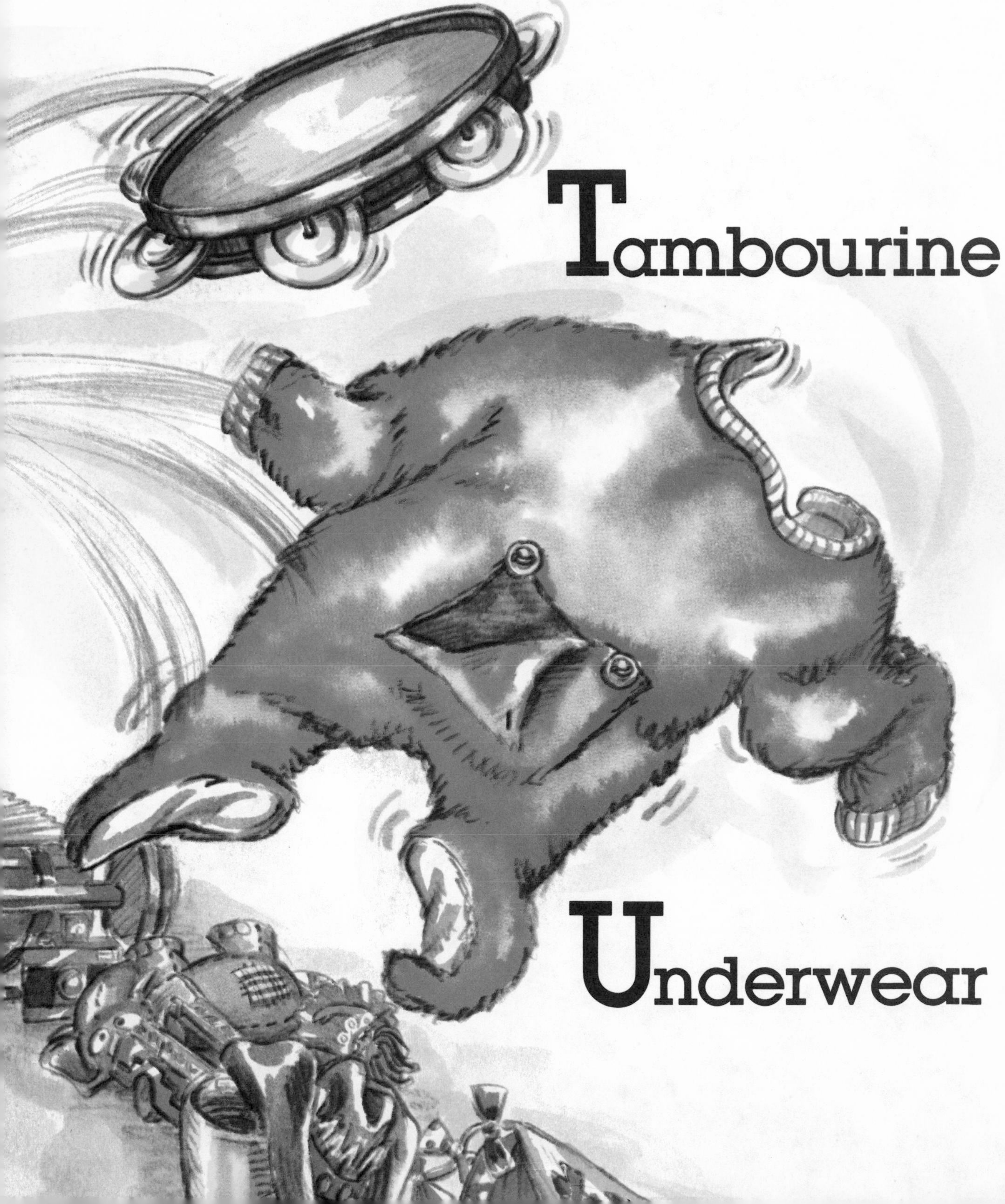

Tambourine

Underwear

Well, now we know it's not his valentine or his watch. Wait. It's probably his xylophone!

Watch

Valentine

Xylophone

Yo-yo

Whoops! It's not his xylophone after all, or his yo-yo. What could it be?

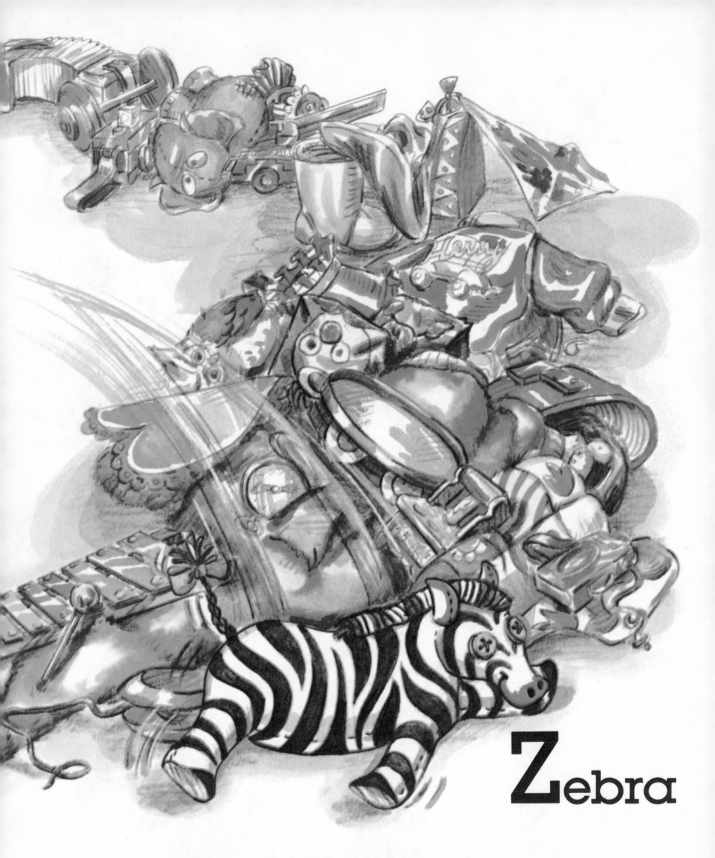

Zebra

It's not his toy zebra.

Look! He's found it!
What is it, Herry? What is it?

Why, it's his Alphabet Book!

Accordion

Barbell

Camera

Doll

Elephant

Fire truck

ABCDEFGHIJ